CIRCUS GIRL

For Seth and Barbara

CIRCUS GIRL

By the author of "The Happy Rain"

JACK SENDAK

Pictures by

MAURICE SENDAK

HARPER  COLLINS

TEXT COPYRIGHT © 1957 BY JACK SENDAK, COPYRIGHT RENEWED 1985 BY JACK SENDAK
PICTURES COPYRIGHT © 1957 BY MAURICE SENDAK, COPYRIGHT RENEWED 1985 BY MAURICE SENDAK
LIBRARY OF CONGRESS CATALOG CARD NUMBER: 57-9258
Manufactured in China.
FOR INFORMATION ADDRESS HARPERCOLLINS CHILDREN'S BOOKS, A DIVISION OF HARPERCOLLINS
PUBLISHERS, 10 EAST 53RD STREET, NEW YORK, NY 10022.
10 11 12 13 SCP 10 9 8 7 6 5 4 3

Flora was a little circus girl. She had been born in the circus—among the glittery lights and the shimmery music. And her friends were the strange and wonderful circus folk. Little Flora had spent all of her life in this dreamy, happy land of the circus, and she found joy in every minute of it.

But then Flora had a terrible dream about the people who came to see the circus every night. She began to wonder what they were like and what they did when they were not at the circus.

One day, as Flora was turning cartwheels with one of the acrobats, she said, "The people who come to see us every night—what do they do when they are not here?"

The acrobat thought for a minute. Then he said, "I hear that they spin on their heads all day long."

"What?" cried Flora.

"That's what I heard," said the acrobat.

Flora was amazed.

"How very very very strange," she said. "How very very very very strange."

Flora walked into the lion's cage. The lion tamer was painting lines on the lion's face to make him look fiercer. The little circus girl put her arm around the lion and watched.

Flora was thinking of the dream she had had. Should she tell the lion tamer about it? The lion licked her fingers.

No—she couldn't do it. Her dream was too frightening. Instead, she said to the lion tamer, "You know, when I was very little, I always used to think that when the audience left every night they turned into clouds of purple smoke. And then, at the next show, they would turn into people again. Wasn't that silly?" Flora giggled.

The lion tamer shrugged.

"I don't know," he said. "Since I haven't heard any different, it might very well be true."

Flora climbed a rope to where the trapeze people were swinging back and forth. When they stopped to rest, she asked, "What are the people on the outside really like?"

And one lady, who was hanging by her toes, said, "They are like spiders."

"What?" cried Flora.

"That's what I heard," said the pretty lady. "They know how to spin webs. And they live in them, all tangled up. The ones that break loose come to see us here at the circus."

Flora did not know what to think. She climbed down and joined the clowns.

"How very very very strange," she said. "How very very very very strange."

"What is the matter, little Flora?" asked one of the clowns. He was pouring water on his head to make his hair grow.

Flora told him what the other circus folk

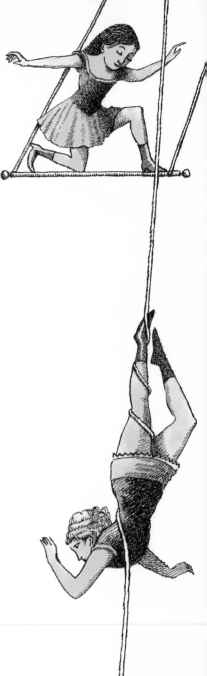

had said about the outside people.

"I don't suppose we'll ever really know," said another clown, who kept falling out of his chair.

But Flora wanted to know. She wanted to know more than anything else in the world. Why was it such a mystery?

She would have to see for herself. She just had to find out how those strange and magical people lived. She had to find out if her awful dream about them was really true.

That very night, Flora slipped out of the circus tent. And when the circus folk saw that she was gone, they sat down on their trunks and waited for her return. And as the shimmery music stopped and the glittery lights went out, the circus folk looked at one another and smiled. They knew deep in their hearts that they were doing the right thing.

Flora ran through the deepening shadows.

"I am so happy," she shouted into the wind. "Now I will find out how the outside people live."

When she came to the village, it was dark and mysterious. There was a heavy mist and the street lights cast strange shadows. Flora's teeth began to chatter. It was all just like her awful dream. Slowly she tiptoed through the streets, trembling at every sound.

Then—she froze with fright. One of the shadows was moving—moving toward her. And before she could run, it sprang forward, growling.

Oh, but it was only a dog. A puppy—a little pepper-colored puppy. And he growled so fiercely that Flora burst into laughter. Imagine! To be so frightened by a puppy! In the circus she played with lions, but here, in this shadowy place, a little dog could frighten her. She hugged him and rubbed her chin on his soft fur.

Flora had a plan. A plan whereby she could watch all that went on in the village without being seen by anyone. With the puppy at her heels, she searched until she found a stout, long rope. Then she climbed up and fastened the rope to the tops of the two tallest trees in the village. It was a difficult job, but Flora managed to get it done without too much trouble.

Carefully, she stepped on the rope and walked across it. And although she had been on a tightrope many times in the circus, Flora was a little uneasy. She had never been so high before, and, of course, there was no net below her. But the little circus girl walked back and forth across the rope—back and forth—back and forth. For this was the best way, the only way, to see how the outside people lived.

The rope trembled beneath her feet, but she tried not to think of it. She tried to imagine instead all the wonderful things she would soon see. And she tried not to think of her dream. It could frighten her too much.

Flora gazed down on the sleeping village. It looked so small. The buildings were like dollhouses—like the ones she played with in the circus.

The puppy was sleeping at the foot of one of the trees. Leaning down, Flora whispered, "I am taller than the houses—taller than the trees. I am just like a giant. With one puff I could blow the whole village into the sky. Did you ever hear of a girl giant? Did you?"

The puppy wagged his tail sleepily.

Flora laughed. Now that she was so high above the village, out of harm's way, she was feeling very happy and brave. And, also, she was especially pleased with herself for having thought of watching the outside people from the tops of the trees. It was such a very very very very good plan.

Flora walked back and forth. It had been a long night. She could hardly wait for the morning to come. To hurry the time away, she began to count chimneys. But when she had counted them all, it was still not morning.

A flock of birds flew by. They circled around her, so close that Flora could see their tiny, shiny eyes. She watched them with delight. Oh, how wonderful it was to fly! And she flapped her arms, pretending she was a bird.

"See—see! I am a bird, too!" she cried to them. "Come—come. Sit on my shoulder."

But the birds flew off, twittering in fright at the strange girl on the tightrope.

Suddenly, the sun peeped over a huge black cloud. And, as the little circus girl watched, the cloud changed from blue to red to magenta to green to yellow. Flora was enchanted.

Then the sun burst into full view—and it was morning, a glorious, sweet-smelling morning. In a way, it reminded her of the circus—when the lights flashed on and the show was about to start.

The first thing she saw was the little pepper-colored puppy. His tail waving impatiently, he was searching for food. Oh, the poor little dog. Was there no one to help him?

Then, all at once, the streets were crowded with people—just like magic. Flora did not know where to look first. In the circus there were three rings where you could watch what you wanted to. But here you didn't know where to look.

The streets were jammed—people walking every which way. Why they didn't all bump into one another Flora could not imagine. Some even read newspapers, but still they seemed to know where they were going. They looked so silly that Flora nearly laughed.

And it was then that Flora realized she could only see the tops of their heads. She could not see their faces.

The little puppy ran among them, barely escaping getting stepped on. But the villagers seemed to take no notice of him. They were too busy doing what they were doing.

But what were they doing down there? They were walking in crazy circles, skipping in and out of buildings, running up and down stairs.

Flora spotted a group of men. They were speaking loudly and joking with one another. But Flora, who could not quite hear them, thought that they must be arguing. She could see them smoking pipes and waving their arms. Perhaps they were magicians, quarreling over what kind of magic spell to make.

Then some children, on their way to school, ran joyously through the streets, playing tag. But Flora, who had never seen that game before, thought they were fighting.

Flora felt very unhappy. She walked back and forth, back and forth across the quivering rope. These outside people were not very nice, she thought. Arguing, fighting, stepping on dogs. They weren't at all like the friendly circus folk.

Flora sat down and covered her eyes with her hands. She did not want to see any more bad things. She was so high up above the outside people that she mistook everything they did. She did not know that what she thought was bad was really not bad at all.

In a little while, though, Flora could not resist peeking through her fingers. Some women stood before their homes, leaning on brooms. Flora shivered. Could they be witches? She recalled the pictures she had seen in books of witches flying through the night air on brooms. Would they fly up and grab her, she wondered. Would they? Of course, they didn't. They were using the brooms only to sweep with.

After that, as the hours went swiftly by, Flora saw many things. But not once did she see anyone spinning on his head, or behaving like a spider, or turning into purple smoke. Really, in spite of all her careful watching, Flora had seen nothing unusual. It was very very very very disappointing.

And she was growing tired. As she walked back and forth across the rope, Flora could hardly make out what was going on below her. She wished she could see their faces.

And then—Flora began to think of her dream. She couldn't help it. It was as though she were dreaming it all over again.

She had dreamed her awful dream on her last birthday. On that very day she had received, as a gift, a rubber stamp of a clown. It was a wonderful present. She remembered how she had pressed the stamp on almost everything in the circus tent. But no matter how often she used it, it always came out the same. The same picture of the clown.

That night, Flora had had her dream about the outside people. She was in their village and a thick mist hung over it. Suddenly, the outside people appeared, and they formed a great, silent circle about her. And as the little circus girl walked around the circle looking at each one of them, she saw that they all had the same face. Men, women and children—all exactly alike. Just as though they had all been stamped with the same rubber stamp. Then, slowly, they closed in around her, staring at her with their dreadful, unmoving eyes.

"Oh, how can they tell who their children are?" cried Flora, as she awoke. "Or who their friends are?"

Ever after that, as Flora stared out into the audience every night, she wondered about her dream—and if it were true. For in the darkness it seemed to her that the faces really were all the same. And that, even though they made laughing sounds, their rubber-stamped faces never changed.

But she wasn't sure. For she was too frightened to get really close to the outside people. The idea that they might all look alike was just too awful.

Many times Flora had wanted to tell her circus friends about the dream. But she didn't—she couldn't. What if they laughed at her? Or called her a baby? No, she couldn't tell them. She had to come and see for herself.

It was growing dark. Flora could hear the little dog whining below her and when she looked down she saw a little girl hugging him and rubbing her chin on his soft fur. Then she went off with him. The stars came out and Flora felt lonely.

She began to cry. She knew she was being silly. But she couldn't help it.

Mostly, she was crying because she was still so uncertain about the outside people. She had set herself so high above the village that she had not been able to see their faces clearly. In fact, she wasn't at all sure about anything she had seen. Oh, if only she had been brave enough to come down from her tree and walk among the outside people. But she hadn't—she couldn't. What if their faces were all the same?

So Flora walked back and forth across the rope, crying. What would she tell the circus folk? Should she tell them that she had seen nothing? Could she tell them that?

At last, when the streets were quite empty, Flora climbed down from the tree. She would go home—to the circus. And she would have to make up a story to tell them about the outside people. She started to run.

But the sound of laughter made her stop. It came from a large house, ablaze with lights. What could be happening now, wondered Flora. Should she look? Should she?

Yes—she would look. And with her heart pounding as though it would burst, Flora ran to the window and looked in.

The room was full of outside people. Even the pepper-colored puppy was there. They were having a party. Flora stood by the window and watched. She could see their faces very clearly. And—wonder of wonders—their faces were not all alike. The outside people were just like the circus folk. They had friendly faces, smiling faces, different faces. Oh, the wonder of it!

In the morning Flora was gone and the cloud that changed colors changed colors alone. High in the sky a flock of birds circled aimlessly. Then the sun burst into full view, and it turned out to be another fine day.

The circus folk were very happy to see Flora again. The lights went on and the shimmery music began to play. And when they asked her what it was like on the outside, Flora said,

"I found out that a dream is nothing but a dream."

"Is that all?" asked the acrobat.

"And I found out that the outside people do not spin on their heads. And that they do not spin webs."

The trapeze lady smiled.

"We knew that too, little Flora," she said. "But we knew that you would want to see for yourself."

"Oh, I know, I know," laughed Flora. "The outside people are just like us. All their faces are different—it's easy for them to tell who their children are. And they have parties. And they play with puppies. Oh, I'm so happy—they are just like us."

The circus folk looked at one another happily. Everything had turned out just right.

Then Flora said, "I think I have a plan."

"Oh, lovely—we just love plans," said the clowns.

"Tonight let us give the outside people the very very very very very best show that we can. Let's give them a show that they will never forget."

The circus folk cheered. It was a wonderful idea.

"Let's start practicing now," shouted the ringmaster.

"Yes. Yes. Let's start practicing now."

Ta-ra-ta-ra-ta-ra blared the trumpets.

And in came the clowns. Stumbling and fumbling and tumbling, making everyone laugh at their nonsense. They were so funny. So lovable. So silly.

And then came the trapeze artists, with their breathtaking tricks and their flying grace. Nothing was too dangerous for them. How daring they were!

Then came the horses—beautiful, white, milky horses. Prancing and snorting. Flora sprang upon one that ran as fast as the wind. Round and round and round they ran.

In came the acrobats, spinning and jumping and turning. There were seven of them standing on one another's shoulders. One atop the other. Then they all came tumbling down. Oh, what a trick that was!

Then the lion roared so loudly that even the lion tamer trembled for his life. And only when the lion winked to show that he was fooling did the tamer recover his usual courage.

Then the clowns set off firecrackers and the tent was filled with shattering noise and blazing color. Dogs jumped through hoops. Elephants danced to the shimmery music. The noise—the smell—the color—it was overpowering. It was glorious. It was beautiful. It was exciting.

Flora and the circus folk shouted with

joy. The outside people would never forget what they saw here.

Round and round and round flew Flora—atop her white horse. Faster and faster and faster. It was so good to be back in the circus with her friends. And tonight she would look out into the audience and there would be no terrible dream to frighten her.

THE END